Treasure Hunt

Look out for more
mermaid adventures:
Spooky Shipwreck
Pirate Trouble
Whale Rescue

Mermaid Rock

Treasure Hunt

Kelly McKain
illustrated by Cecilia Johansson

Scholastic Canada Ltd.

Toronto New York London Auckland Sydney
Mexico City New Delhi Hong Kong Buenos Aires

To Katie, with huggles

Scholastic Canada Ltd.
604 King Street West, Toronto, Ontario M5V 1E1, Canada

Scholastic Inc.
557 Broadway, New York, NY 10012, USA

Scholastic Australia Pty Limited
PO Box 579, Gosford, NSW 2250, Australia

Scholastic New Zealand Limited
Private Bag 94407, Greenmount, Auckland, New Zealand

Scholastic Children's Books
Euston House, 24 Eversholt Street, London NW1 1DB, UK

Library and Archives Canada Cataloguing in Publication
McKain, Kelly
Treasure hunt / Kelly McKain ; illustrated by Cecilia Johansson.
(Mermaid rock)
ISBN 0-439-93538-5 (pbk.)
I. Johansson, Cecilia II. Title. III. Series.
PR6113.C43T47 2007   j823'.92   C2006-903935-6

ISBN-10 0-439-93538-5 / ISBN-13 978-0-439-93538-8

First published in the UK by Scholastic Ltd., 2004.
First Canadian edition published 2007 by Scholastic Canada Ltd.

Text copyright © Kelly McKain, Prospero Promotions Limited, 2004.
Illustrations copyright © Cecilia Johansson, 2004.
All rights reserved.

6 5 4 3 2 1   Printed in Singapore   07 08 09 10 11

It was an ordinary day on Mermaid Rock.
Coralie and Shelle were singing and
combing their hair.

"Come on, Spirulina, join in!" they cried.

"But it's boring," grumbled Spirulina.

"I wish I could have an adventure instead."

WHOOSH!

Suddenly a chariot pulled by two giant sea horses came thundering towards them.

"It's Father!" Spirulina cried.

Neptune's chariot skidded to a halt, splashing his three daughters from top to tail.

Spirulina giggled – she loved sea spray. But she soon stopped laughing when she saw the sad look on Neptune's face.

"Oh, my darlings, I bring terrible news," he boomed. "I lost a bet with Ariel and now I must give him all my treasure."

The three sisters gasped with horror.

"No treasure?" cried Coralie.

Neptune hung his proud head. "It's even worse than that. My treasure's been stolen! Now Ariel says that I must find it by sunset or he'll take the Floating Palace instead."

"No palace?" shouted Shelle.
Spirulina's sisters began to scream
and sob.

"What terrible news, Father!"
said Spirulina. "But don't
worry. I'll find the
treasure before sunset.
You won't have to
give the Floating
Palace to Ariel."
Neptune hugged
Spirulina tenderly.

"My brave little one," he said, "you mean well, but what can you do? You are only a fragile mermaid. I shall go and prepare to leave my beloved palace."

With that, he leaped aboard his chariot and swept off over the sea.

"He's right," wept Shelle. "There's nothing you can do."

"We'll see about that," grumbled Spirulina, who did not like being called little or fragile. "The treasure must be hidden somewhere."

9

She stood up on her tail and looked around, but all she could see from Mermaid Rock was a broken fishing rod on the beach.

Just then, she glanced up and spotted Ariel's Sky Castle, floating high above on its cloud.

"I bet I could see for miles from one of those turrets," Spirulina cried. "I'd be sure to spot the stolen treasure then."

"But how will you get up there?"
asked Coralie. "Mermaids
can't fly!"

"Wait and see," said
Spirulina, winking.

She swam over to the shore and collected
the broken fishing rod. Then she fetched her
tool belt and set to
work. Soon it
was as good
as new.

Spirulina swam back to Mermaid Rock
and showed the rod to her sisters: "I'll hook
the Sky Castle with this
rod," she explained.
"Then I'll reel
myself up."

"Don't be stupid,
Spirulina!" snickered Shelle.
"You'll never manage that!" cried Coralie.

☆ Chapter Two ☆

Spirulina stood on the very tip of Mermaid Rock and cast up at the Sky Castle. But no matter how hard she tried, the fishing line wouldn't go high enough. Even worse, the Sky Castle had nearly floated out of reach.

"It won't work!"
shouted Shelle.

"Give up now!"
called Coralie.

But Spirulina kept
on trying until…

"Yes!" She was suddenly pulled into the
sky! She looked up and gasped in surprise…

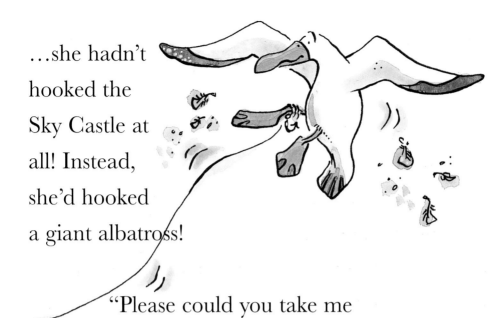

…she hadn't
hooked the
Sky Castle at
all! Instead,
she'd hooked
a giant albatross!

"Please could you take me
to the Sky Castle," she called.

"I'm not taking you
anywhere," said the
albatross crossly.
"In fact, I'm
going to shake
you off in a
minute. I'm not
a taxi service,
you know."

Spirulina gulped as she swung around on the fishing line. It was a very long way down. She felt very frightened.

"Oh, please help me," she cried. "I'm on an important mission. You see, someone has stolen my father's treasure. I must find it before sunset!"

"My, that really is important," said the albatross. "Okay, climb aboard and I'll take you to the Sky Castle. You can call me Albi."

"I'm Spirulina," panted Spirulina, scrambling onto Albi's back. She hooked the fishing line onto her tool belt.

A few moments later they reached the Sky Castle. "Hold on tight," called Albi. "It might be a bumpy landing!"

With a crash and a bang, Spirulina and Albi touched down on top of one of the turrets.

Ariel, who had been busy inside the castle, heard all the noise and flew out to see what was happening.

"What are you two doing up here?" he demanded.

"We're looking for the stolen treasure," Spirulina explained. "You don't mind, do you?"

Ariel laughed. "Mind? Of course not! Good luck to you!" And with that, he flew back inside.

Spirulina and Albi grinned at each other, and started the search for the stolen treasure.

☆ Chapter Three ☆

Spirulina and Albi hurried from tower to tower, looking in every direction. They peered far out to sea and all along the coast, but there was no sign of the stolen treasure.

"Oh, dear!" said Spirulina. "I really thought we would see it from up here."

"Don't worry," said Albi. "Let's fly around and take a closer look."

Albi's idea made Spirulina feel much more cheerful.

They swooped down off the turret…

…and checked the upturned fishing boats and the lighthouse, but there was no stolen treasure.

They searched all day,
peering deep inside
craggedy caves…

…and digging up sandy beaches in case
the stolen treasure had been buried.

But there was no sign of it anywhere.

Just as the sun was beginning to set, Spirulina and Albi landed on top of the Sky Castle once again. They took one last sweeping look, but there was still no sign of the stolen treasure. They were both exhausted, filthy and utterly miserable.

Just then, Ariel flew up to them.

"Have you found the treasure yet?"
he asked.

"No,"
Albi admitted.

"Oh, what a
shame!" said Ariel.

But instead of being sad, he looked
delighted.

"I will have to take the Floating Palace
instead."

"Please, Ariel, don't take my father's home," begged Spirulina, starting to cry.

But Ariel just laughed.

"A bet is a bet. Now, excuse me. It's only a few minutes till sunset. I have to get to Mermaid Rock to claim my new palace."

"What a wicked sprite!" squawked Albi, when Ariel had flown away. "But it looks like the palace will be his after all. We've searched everywhere! We'll have to give up."

"Don't say that!" said Spirulina, drying her eyes. "We must keep looking."

As the sun sank lower it shone straight onto the Sky Castle.

Suddenly Spirulina spotted something glinting in the tiny, barred window opposite.

"Look over there!" she gasped.
"I think I can see
something."

Albi peered at the window. "It's probably
nothing," he squawked sadly, "but climb
aboard, and
we'll take
a closer
look."

Hardly daring to hope, Spirulina and Albi swooped across to the window, landed on the wide ledge and peered inside.

Chapter Four

"Father's treasure!" cried Spirulina.

"Shh!" hissed Albi.

There was a mean-looking guard sitting right next to the pile of jewels. Spirulina and Albi ducked down just as the guard turned around.

"Ariel stole the treasure himself!" whispered Spirulina crossly. "What a sneak!"

"But why would he do that?" whispered Albi. "He's won it anyway."

Spirulina thought hard. "Yes, but this way he gets the Floating Palace too! Then he'll rule the sky and the sea. He'll banish Father forever. Oh, Albi, we have to stop him!"

"You're right!" squawked Albi. "We must
rescue the treasure – and
fast! The sun has almost
set! But we can't
get in through
these bars."

Albi looked defeated, but Spirulina
grinned. "We can't. But this can," she said,
unclipping the fishing rod from her tool belt.

"Good idea!" squawked Albi. "We can fish for it! But how can we get rid of that guard?"

"Leave it to me," said Spirulina. "For once, my boring old mermaid skills will come in useful."

Spirulina leaned close to the window and began to sing softly.

Go to sleep, go to sleep, go to sleep, you big old guard. You are snoring, you are snoring, to this boring mermaid song.

Spirulina sang the song over and over. Soon the guard fell into a deep slumber.

"Wow, how did you do that?" asked Albi.

"Mermaid lullabies send humans to sleep," Spirulina explained. "Okay, time to go fishing."

She cast the line through the window, snagged a pearl necklace and reeled it in.

CLINK!

The necklace hit the iron bars. Spirulina froze, afraid that the guard would wake up. But he just snorted and went back to his dreams.

35

Piece by piece, Spirulina pulled the
treasure out of the window
and piled it onto Albi's
back.

"The…sun…has…almost…set…"
panted Albi, struggling to balance under
the weight of the treasure.
"H…h…hurry!"

"Just one more
thing," said
Spirulina, casting
off into the
gloomy room.

Spirulina heaved at the line. "This
diamond tiara is very heavy," she panted.
"That's…no…diamond…tiara…"
gasped Albi.

Quick as a flash, Spirulina grabbed the
tiara, stuck out her tongue at the guard and
leaped onto Albi's
back.
"Let's go!"
she cried.

As the guard raced towards them, Albi launched off the windowsill and flapped his wings as hard as he could. But instead of zooming away, they just hung in the air. The treasure was far too heavy.

"Ahhhhh!" they screamed, spiralling downwards.

While Spirulina was busy rescuing the treasure, Ariel had arrived on Mermaid Rock, to claim his winnings.

"Spirulina hasn't found the stolen treasure," he told Neptune, "even though I was kind enough to let her look from the Sky Castle. So you must give me the Floating Palace instead."

Neptune's shoulders drooped as he pulled
a chain from his thick belt. The chain held
the keys to the Floating Palace. Coralie wept
and Shelle wailed

as the sun
vanished
from the
sky.

But just as Neptune was about to hand
over the keys…it began raining treasure!

"Hooray! The treasure is found!" cried
Coralie as diamond tiaras, pearl necklaces
and sapphire rings fell around them.

"Father, the palace is saved!" squealed Shelle.

But Neptune was staring up at the sky in horror. "My little one!" he croaked.

Spirulina and Albi were falling fast, heading straight for a crash landing on Mermaid Rock.

Albi flapped hard, but they kept falling.

"I'm going to dive into the sea," cried Spirulina, "then you'll be able to fly out of harm's way!"

"No!" squawked Albi. "It's too dangerous!"

"Don't worry, I'll be fine," said Spirulina, although she felt really frightened.

She crossed her
fingers for
luck and then
leaped off
Albi's back.
SPLASH!

Spirulina bobbed to the surface just as Albi landed safely nearby.

Neptune beamed with relief. Coralie and Shelle clapped their hands in delight.

"Oh, my daughter, thank goodness you're safe!" bellowed Neptune. He bent down over the water and lifted Spirulina up in his strong arms.

"And you found the treasure!" cried Coralie. "Just in time!"

"It was Albi too," said Spirulina.

"Well done, both of you," boomed Neptune. "But who stole it?"

"He did!" cried Spirulina, pointing at Ariel. "It was a trick to get the Floating Palace!"

"WHAT?" roared Neptune.

Ariel backed away from the furious sea king. "I m-m-must be going now," he stammered, and flew off.

"I'll deal
with him later,"
Neptune promised.
"Tonight there
will be a party
in honour of
Spirulina and her
new friend, Albi!"

Coralie and Shelle cheered and hurried
off to tell all the creatures of the sea.

The party was held at the
Floating Palace. There was
music and dancing, fireworks
and a huge cake.

Neptune raised a goblet of fruit punch.
"A toast!" he bellowed, "to Albi and my
brave daughter, Spirulina!"

"To Albi and Spirulina!" everyone cried.

Albi squawked with happiness, but Spirulina just smiled and sipped her punch, wondering what exciting adventures tomorrow would bring.